The Mountain Who
Wanted to Live in a House

For my grandchildren
– Maurice Shadbolt

The Mountain Who Wanted to Live in a House

By Maurice Shadbolt

Illustrated by Renee Haggo

STARFISH BAY
CHILDREN'S BOOKS

Once there was a mountain who lived all by itself.

Sometimes people came to climb it. In winter they came to ski and make snowmen. In summer they came to have picnics and watch the birds in the trees.

But did anyone ask the mountain how it liked living high in the sky?

No one ever did.

As a matter of fact, the mountain wanted to live in a house.

Every day the mountain looked down at people in a town. They all went home at night to their houses. They weren't cold and lonely. They were out of the snow and rain and wild wind, with other people.

But the mountain just had to go right on being a mountain, up in the cold clouds, without a house to live in.

So one day the mountain made up its mind. With a 'Woho, woho' kind of laugh it walked toward the town.

No one had ever seen anything like it before. A mountain walking? But it was. It walked toward the town with a rumbling, tumbling sound.

Birds flew away. The cold clouds fell off the mountain with a thump. The trees fell down with a bump.

The people in the town were frightened. They drove away in their cars. They rowed away in their boats. Or they just ran as fast as they could, away from the town, away from the walking mountain.

The mountain felt sad. It didn't want people to run away. It only wanted to be friendly and warm inside a house. Didn't anyone understand?

No one did. They just kept running and rowing and driving away.

Everyone had gone except a boy called Thomas. No one had told Thomas he ought to be frightened of a mountain walking with a "Woho, woho" kind of laugh.

So Thomas just stood all by himself and watched the mountain walk closer and closer and become bigger and bigger, until he could hardly see its top.

"Hey!" Thomas shouted. "What do you think you're doing?"

The mountain stopped walking, very surprised, and looked down at tiny Thomas.

"Stop it at once," Thomas said. "Mountains mustn't go walking around. You're scaring all the birds and crushing all the trees."

"Where has everybody gone?" asked the mountain.

"I think they're frightened of you," Thomas said.

"Frightened?" the mountain asked. "Frightened? Am I so ugly that I frighten people?" Two big patches of snow on its face melted and fell, like two large tears, and rolled off the mountainside—plip, plip, plop—and made two little lakes at Thomas's feet.

Thomas tried to make the mountain feel better. "You're a beautiful mountain when you're high in the sky," he said. "Not when you're walking around though. People aren't used to mountains walking around."

"But I only want to be like people," the mountain said. "I only want to live in a house."

"Live in a house?" said Thomas, who knew that mountains couldn't live in houses. Mountains were much, much too big.

"Can't you help?" the mountain asked. "Can't you help me live in a house?"

"No one ever built a house as big as a mountain," Thomas said sensibly because he was a sensible boy.

The mountain became fidgety and walked around with a rumbling, tumbling sound.

"Please stop that," Thomas said, "or you'll give me a headache. I'm trying to think how to make you small."

"Small?" said the mountain, most surprised.

"Small so you'll fit in a house," Thomas explained. "Sometimes when my mother washes my clothes, they shrink. I'll wash you and see if you shrink. Just stay where you are for a minute."

Thomas ran home and fetched soap, lots of soap, and a scrubbing brush, and then he got to work. He scrubbed the mountain with the brush and soap, and the soap bubbles flew everywhere. He scrubbed and scrubbed, all up one side of the mountain and down the other. He scrubbed until his arms ached, until he was too tired to stand up, until the brush was worn out and all the soap was gone.

"Oh dear," said the mountain, all wet and bubbly. "Oh dear." And it sneezed, "Ah-tish-ah-tish-OOOooo," the biggest sneeze anyone in the world had ever heard, so that all the bubbles blew away in the breeze. Thomas nearly blew away, too. And the mountain hadn't shrunk. It was still as big as ever, far too big to live in a house.

"We'll have to try something else to make you small," Thomas decided. He ran home to get his father's hammer. He climbed up the side of the mountain and began hitting at it with the hammer, so that bits of rock began falling down.

"OW-ow-OW, what are you doing?" the mountain yelled.

"Making you smaller," Thomas said. "Don't you want to live in a house?" And Thomas went on hammering away, with sore hands and aching arms, trying to help the mountain fit in a house.

"Please stop," said the mountain. "If you keep breaking bits off me, I won't be a mountain anymore. If I stop being a mountain, I won't be anything anymore."

Thomas hadn't thought of that. So he stopped hammering. As soon as he stopped he had a new idea.

"My father," he said, "is an artist. He could paint a picture of you to fit in a house. That wouldn't hurt a bit. And you could go right on being a mountain. If you don't go back to where you belong, where will the trees live, and the birds? And where will people have picnics in summer and ski and make snowmen in winter?"

The mountain began looking happy again. "That way," Thomas said, "you can live in a house and be a mountain, too. Hurry back to where you belong, as fast as you can, and I'll find my father."

So the mountain hurried away, with a "Woho woho" kind of laugh and a rumbling, tumbling sound.

Thomas ran to his father. "I promised you would paint a picture of the mountain so it can live in a house."

"Of course," said his father, who was really glad to find Thomas wasn't hurt and had been so brave and sensible.

So Thomas and his father found a comfortable place to sit near the mountain, and his father began to paint a picture.

"You must help too," his father said, and gave Thomas a brush. "You paint the clouds, and I'll paint the sky." And together Thomas and his father painted the mountain.

While they painted, Thomas thought he saw the mountain give him a wink and a secret smile. He was sure, too, that he heard a "Woho, woho" kind of laugh flying high away in the wind.

When they finished the picture, Thomas carried it home and hung it above the fireplace where everyone could see it. And that was how the mountain managed to live in a house and go right on being a mountain, too.